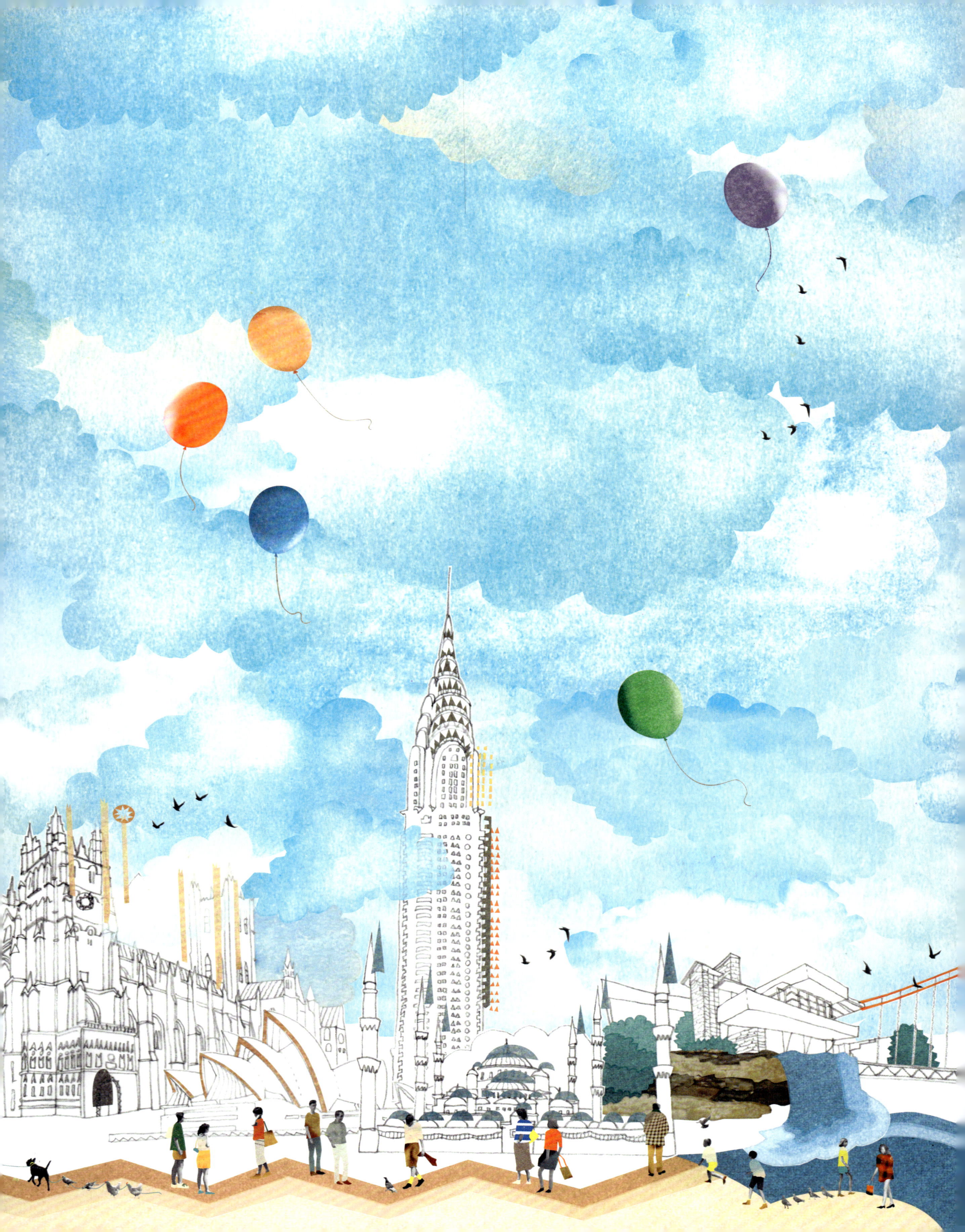

ARCHITECTURE ACCORDING TO PIGEONS

by Speck Lee Tailfeather

Surprised to see a book written by a pigeon? Of course you are! And who can blame you? These days, humans are brought up to believe that we are nothing but dirty, disease-carrying vermin. You probably know almost nothing of the ancient history between our two species; of how, for many centuries, you humans relied on us to deliver your most important messages. And in return you treated us with great respect, building us wonderful homes and bringing us tasty titbits for our tea.

But now that the telephone and the internet have come along, we are no longer as useful to you. Now, humans call pest controllers to poison us; you stick spikes on the window ledges we try to perch on, and allow your small children to chase us.

This turn of affairs saddens us deeply. It is why, at a recent meeting of Pigeon Elders, it was decided that the time has come to reveal the truth about our species — to show humans that pigeons are gentle and intelligent creatures.

It's time to tell you about our deep and abiding passion for architecture. That's right! We love your beautiful buildings! Why else do you think we flock about them in such great numbers, risking your violence towards us?

And so it was that I, Speck Lee Tailfeather, was elected by my peers as the pigeon to make this secret known and approach renowned publisher Phaidon Press. Fortunately, our gamble paid off. Phaidon agreed to make this beautiful book, and I embarked on a trip around the world to visit some of its most remarkable buildings and structures. Here is a chronicle of my journey, with a little of what I know about architecture thrown in. It is my dearest hope that, by the end of our trip, you will not only have caught some of our buzz for buildings, but also realize that there is more — so much more! — to pigeons than you could ever have imagined. Read on, my friend, read on...

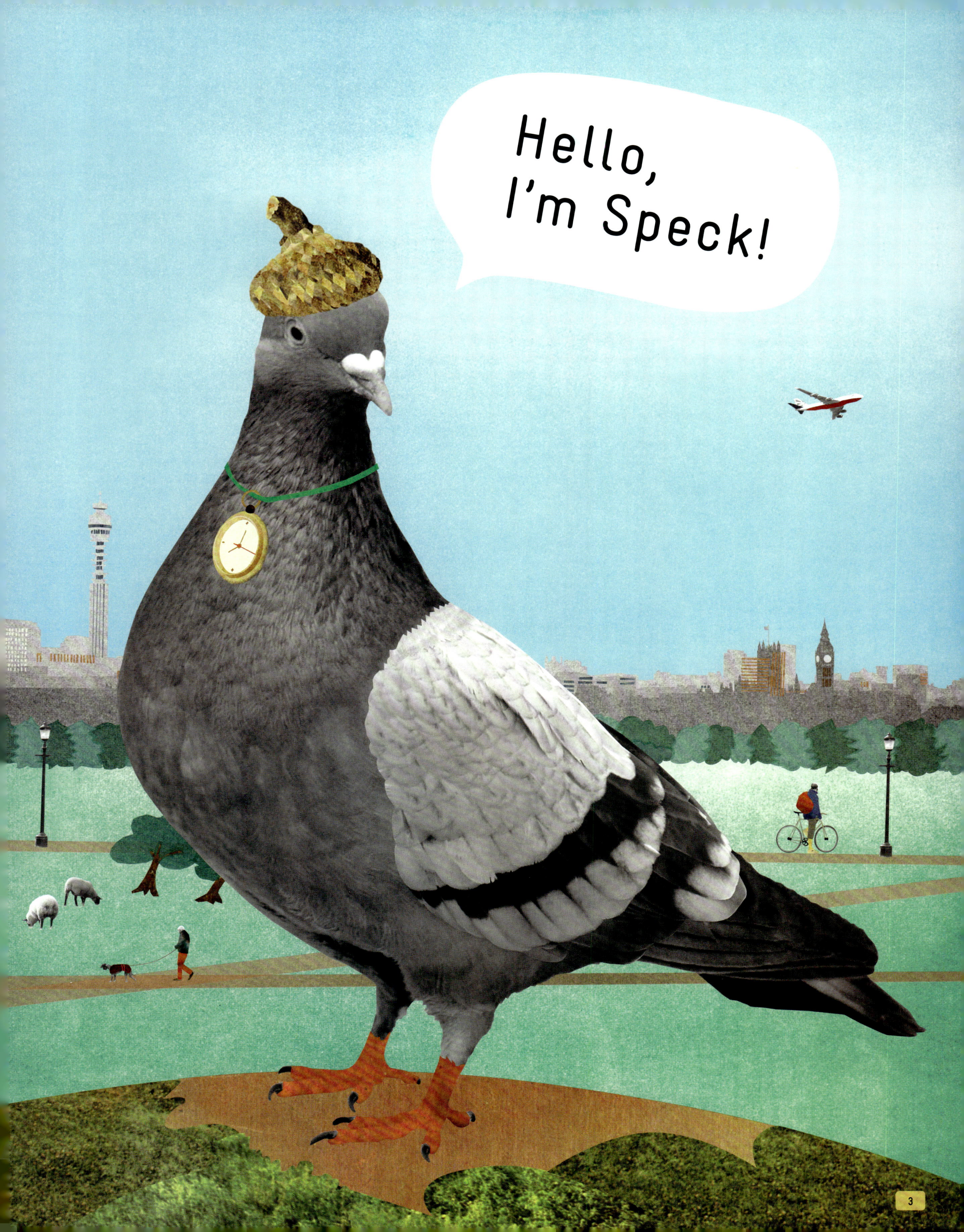
Hello,
I'm Speck!

Here are the beauties I'm planning to take you to – each is called by its pigeon name with your human name underneath. Now come along, come along!

THE MISH-MASH MARVEL
a.k.a Canterbury Cathedral
pages 6–7

THE IRON TREE
a.k.a Eiffel Tower
pages 8–9

GUTS GALLERY
a.k.a Georges Pompidou Centre
pages 10–11

THE FOREST OF DREAMS
a.k.a Basilica de la Sagrada Familia
pages 14–17

THE CRABSHELL
a.k.a Notre-Dame de Ronchamp
pages 12–13

THE WATERY WARREN
a.k.a Venice
pages 18–19

THE FLOATING FANCY
a.k.a San Giorgio Maggiore
pages 20–21

MURDER RING
a.k.a Colosseum
pages 22–25

BUILDING BRIDGES
pages 26–29

4 CONTENTS

THE MYSTERIOUS MATHEMATICAL MIRACLE
a.k.a Great Pyramid of Giza
pages 30–31

THE PALACE OF GHOSTS
a.k.a Taj Mahal
pages 32–35

THE GREAT WORM
a.k.a Great Wall of China
pages 36–37

THE LITTLE GREY BOX
a.k.a Church of the Light
pages 38–39

HUNGRY BEAKS HALL
a.k.a Sydney Opera House
pages 40–41

THE BIG BIRD
a.k.a Brasilia
pages 42–45

MY BEST TOWERS EVER
pages 46–49

FALLINGWATER
a.k.a Fallingwater – our pigeon name for the building is the same!
pages 50–53

KING OF THE CASTLES
a.k.a Chrysler Building
pages 54–55

THE SILVER SQUIGGLE
a.k.a Walt Disney Concert Hall
pages 56–57

... and to learn more about each building and its architect, have a look at pages 60–63

THE MISH-MASH MARVEL
a.k.a. Canterbury Cathedral

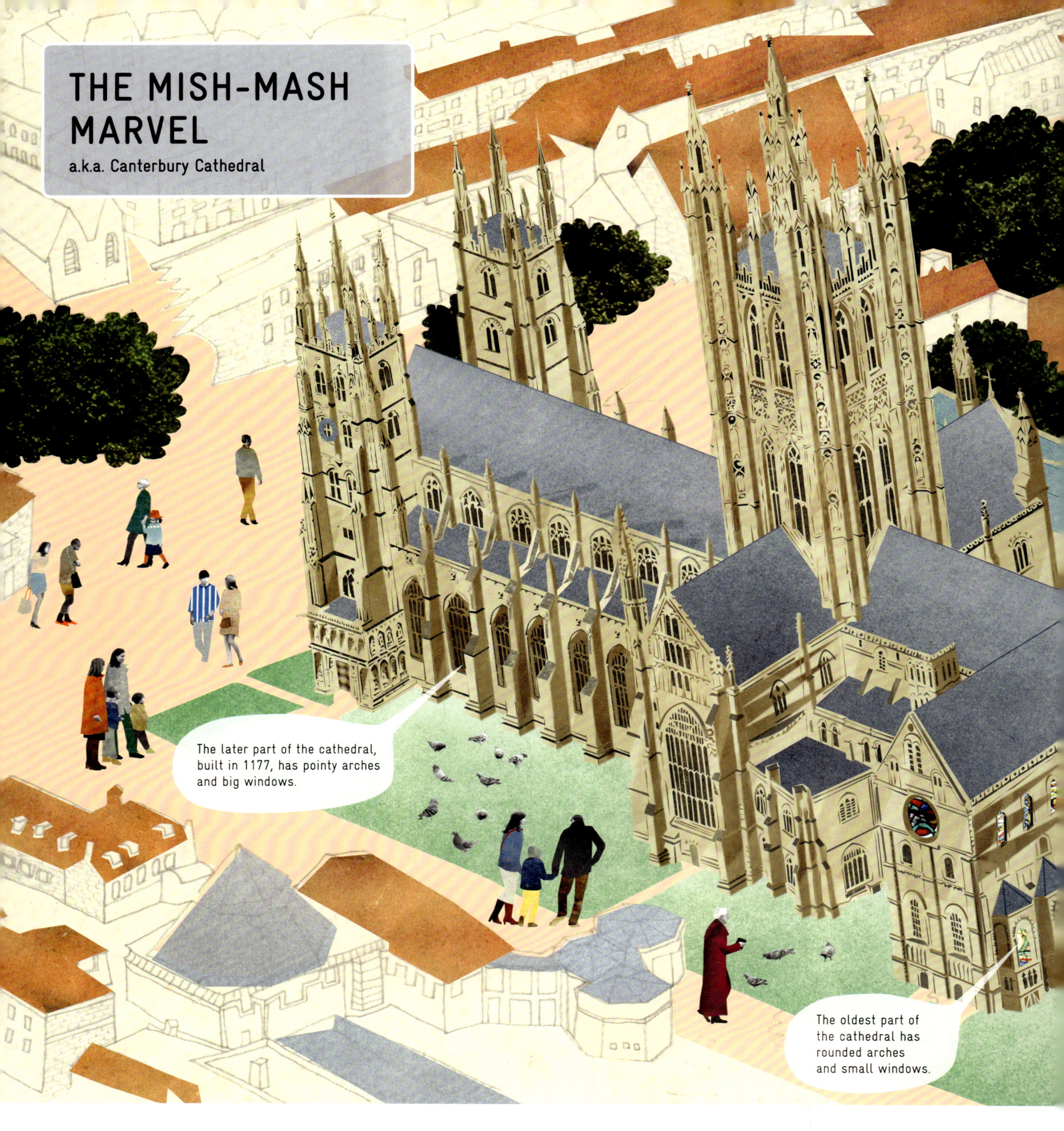

The later part of the cathedral, built in 1177, has pointy arches and big windows.

The oldest part of the cathedral has rounded arches and small windows.

Off I set, on the first leg of my journey, beaked for the south-east coast of England. Sorry as I was to leave my dear Elsie and my friends, I felt a rush of excitement at what was before me, for what more exciting building could there be to begin my travels with than Canterbury flappin' Cathedral?

The whole point of a cathedral, you see, is to fill the visitor with awe and wonder at the glories of heaven – as well as fear of the horrors of hell. A cathedral is basically a massive medieval special effect, like the most stomach-churning moment you have ever had in a 3D film, but in stone and stained glass.

The tall, knobbled spires of the enormous cathedral were visible from a long way off. As I flapped in over the city on a sea-flavoured breeze, sunlight flashed across the enormous stained-glass windows and I felt a thrill of anticipation.

First started in 597, the Cathedral has been rebuilt and added to many times over the centuries and in many different styles. The Cathedral's Archbishop is head of the Church of England, a position that for hundreds of years held almost as much power as the monarch. So, over the centuries, every new

> Standing in the cathedral, looking up into the beautiful Bell Harry Tower, you see the vaulted columns fanning out in a glorious shell-like pattern that frames a tiny, star-like cross in its centre.

> Each stained-glass window is like a mini-movie in itself, depicting jewel-bright tales of knights and saints.

Archbishop has wanted to put his own stamp on the cathedral – to mark their territory, if you will, rather like the way dogs widdle on lampposts, only considerably more elegant.

Canterbury Cathedral is always busy with hundreds of tourists but I managed to hop in through the ancient wooden doors at the front and shelter under a pew. Wow! Fully overawed! The special effects practically jumped out at me as I wandered around. There were so many amazing things, I hardly knew where to look ... In the crypt, I came face-to-face with a hideous monster. Fortunately, it turned out to be a very life-like stone statue, conjured up by medieval stone-masons to strike the terror of hell into the hearts of the faithful. When I encountered an enormous bronze lectern (or book stand) shaped like an eagle crouched ready for flight, my senses got the better of me – I couldn't take any more of the cathedral's drama. Staggering from the doors, I felt quite overcome, and had to sit down to rest on the gravestone of a Mrs P. Spurgeon for a good while afterwards. Canterbury Cathedral is so magnificent, it nearly made me faint – now how many buildings can you say *that* about?

THE IRON TREE
a.k.a Eiffel Tower

The third floor is a popular viewing spot for tourists.

Every one of its 18,038 pieces of iron is bolted firmly together with massive screws called rivets.

After sunset, the tower fizzes with hundreds of tiny lights every hour for five minutes. It also has a huge beacon at the top that sweeps across Paris, like a giant lighthouse.

The lifts that carry you up the tower were one of the most difficult parts to create, because they have to tilt slightly to travel along the arc of the pillars.

When it's windy, the tower can sway by up to 15 centimetres!

THE IRON TREE A.K.A EIFFEL TOWER

> The four pillars supporting the tower align with the compass: north, south, east and west.

Now to me, the Eiffel Tower says 'Paris' and 'France', just like an overflowing bin of burger wrappings says 'lunch'. Funny how a single structure can come to represent so much – like the Statue of Liberty for New York, or Big Ben for London – the Eiffel Tower has become the symbol for a whole city and even a whole country.

I spent a comfortable night snuggled in the eaves of a hotel overlooking the River Seine, which gave me a great view of 'la Tour Eiffel'. All lit up, it looked wonderfully dramatic, soaring above the Paris skyline. The next morning, after breakfasting behind a favourite little café of mine, I flew Eiffel-wards through a crisp, blue sky. The latticed tower looked almost delicate, like spun sugar in a cake shop. But when I got up close and perched high, looking over the city, I could see that it's as solid as a hawk's claw. Each iron beam criss-crosses another, and each time they cross, it strengthens the tower against the pulling-down force of gravity as well as the pushing-sideways force of the wind.

And what a wind! The gales up there really ruffled the old feathers! Not surprising, really, because it's huge: for over forty years, this was the tallest man-made structure in the whole world. It was built as a magnificent gateway, would you believe, for the 1889 World's Fair. Imagine walking under that!

In fact, Gustave Eiffel, the architect, was known as the 'magician of iron' for his daring new ideas. Instead of creating an iron skeleton to support the skin of the structure, here, the iron skeleton IS the structure! Everything is laid bare for you to see – nothing is hidden or dressed up. For me, this honesty is beautiful.

However the tower's stark appearance was so unusual at the time that many Parisians thought it was a monstrosity, spoiling their beautiful city. It was actually only planned to stand for twenty years after the World's Fair, but then the government realized it could be used as a radio communications tower during the First World War and it was allowed to stay. Now of course it's such a part of Paris that you can hardly imagine the city without it.

GUTS GALLERY
(a.k.a Georges Pompidou Centre)

The Pompidou houses not only a big museum of modern art but also a public library, conference and performance spaces, children's play areas and restaurants.

The steel skeleton that supports the whole building stands on the outside like scaffolding.

Ah, gay Paris, city of lovers. Elsie and I came here when we were first a-courting. Fluttering flirtishly over a croissant in the gutter; billing on pretty wrought-iron balconies ... happy days. It all came flooding back as I took a leisurely flap over Paris earlier this afternoon, towards the Pompidou Centre, or 'Beaubourg' as the locals call it, named after the neighbourhood it stands in.

Built in 1973, the Pompidou really is an extraordinary-looking building. It's a bit like something from a sci-fi movie that's landed amidst the old, grey stone townhouses in Paris's centre. And indeed, word on the wing is that its architects (Richard Rogers and Renzo Piano) wanted to turn traditional ideas about architecture inside out, creating a hi-tech building for the future. The President of France had asked that they create a building with as much public space as possible, so they came up with the idea of turning the building itself inside out, and putting everything that usually goes on the inside ... on the outside. Staircases and corridors, plumbing and heating pipes: all the things that would usually be hidden are there for all to see.

Everything that makes the building work is visible, painted in bright colours to say what it is. The structure is white; plumbing pipes are green; blue pipes are for heating and ventilation; yellow is for electric cables; and anything painted red is for movement and safety, such as the escalators and fire extinguishers.

Escalators travel up the side of the building, giving great views over the city of Paris.

The square gives the people and pigeons of Paris somewhere to sit and stroll about in an otherwise very built-up area.

The architects' clever, inside-out design created so much room that they even managed to leave space for a lovely, open square in front of the Pompidou.

Cruising above, I see again how the building wears its guts entirely exposed for everyone to see. Elsie didn't like it much – she called it an ugly eyesore, spoiling her pretty Paris. And she was not alone. Lots of Parisians agreed with her at first. Personally, I like the contrast it makes – the new against the old – as well as its honesty: again, like the Eiffel Tower, it really has nothing to hide.

After a waddle around the square, I seized a chance to flutter up and perch on the moving handrail of one of the escalators that run up the side of the building. Woo hoo! As I climbed higher, I could see the Eiffel Tower and the church of Sacre Cœur in the distance. Some of the other passengers riding with me were tourists, but most were Parisians – exactly the people the Pompidou was built for. This building was created to give local people a big space to enjoy wonderful art and whatever you think about the way it looks (what *do* you think, by the way?), that is surely a beautiful thing.

11

THE CRABSHELL
a.k.a Notre-Dame de Ronchamp

> Because the walls are so thick, the windows have very deep windowsills that angle out, to allow in as much natural light as possible. And because the windows are coloured, the light that streams through is coloured too.

> The space between the roof and the walls allows more natural light into the church.

I reached Notre-Dame de Ronchamp, a chapel built in 1954 in Eastern France, around mid-afternoon today, as heavy, grey storm clouds were building. I almost couldn't believe my beady blinkers! This was like no church I'd ever seen before. That roof! It's like a sweep of joy up to the heavens! Like the curve of my own wing, wheeling in the blue. I swooped down for a closer look and saw that this roof, though built of heavy concrete, seems to magically float – or maybe even billow – above the walls. The gap between the wall and the roof was just wide enough for a l'il ole pigeon to perch in, and from where I was waddling, I could see that the roof is supported by columns hidden in the wall. Very clever.

The white walls swell and curve softly as if they have grown from the earth: in some places they are 1.2 metres thick, in others as wide as 3 metres, and there isn't a straight line to be seen. Le Corbusier, the architect, wanted his church to reflect the gently curving horizon of the surrounding countryside.

This peaceful little chapel sits on the highest point of a hill with green woodland falling away on every side – up here, it feels like there's nothing betwixt you and the

12   THE CRABSHELL A.K.A NOTRE-DAME DE RONCHAMP

When it rains, the water runs off the roof down a specially designed channel. It gushes and gurgles on to sculptures below to make a beautiful rain fountain.

The chapel is small, but has an outdoor pulpit for festival days when people can't all squeeze inside.

Big Guy in the Sky. Unlike some churches, which are very grand and dramatic, this is a calm, gentle place that fits well with its country setting.

The main door is one enormous concrete slab, decorated with coloured shapes, which pivots on a rod in its centre and swings open to create two entrances. I managed to sneak in on one side as someone was leaving on the other, and realized I had the place to myself! Fluttering up, I just about managed to perch on one of the many steep windowsills that dot the south wall. At that moment, the sun pierced the clouds outside, and light streamed through the coloured glass of the windows, staining the white walls opposite with jewel-bright washes of colour.

Notre-Dame de Ronchamp is almost like a sculpture: a work of art in itself. It reflects its natural surroundings, its history and its use as a place of prayer and thought. I haven't liked some of Le Corbusier's other buildings – which look very different to this, often built in rectangular plain concrete blocks –, but I really loved Ronchamp. What an unexpected treat!

13

THE FOREST OF DREAMS
a.k.a Basilica de la Sagrada Família

Sagrada Família has only been used as a church since 2010, not very long, considering it has been worked on since 1882!

Everywhere you look, there are stone carvings and sculptures so delicate that they appear to ripple and drip from the walls and ceilings, or bloom suddenly into fantastical shapes, before dissolving back again into the solid froth.

14 THE FOREST OF DREAMS A.K.A BASILICA DE LA SAGRADA FAMILIA

And so to Spain and Sagrada Familia. I'd heard that the basilica was pretty amazing, but nothing prepared me for just *how* amazing. It has tree-trunk columns and melted-cheese arches that twist and taper into shapes so fanciful they could be from a dream.

There is a great sense of fun, almost enchantment, about it, and yet this is a church: a sacred, serious building. Its architect, the genius Antoni Gaudí, certainly took it seriously, making sure that its tallest spire would be 1 metre shorter than the highest hill nearby, so that he did not outdo God's work.

It's a trickier building than most to get a perch on, because it's still not actually finished. There are cranes, netting and grumpy builders everywhere. But as evening falls, the cranes become still, and Sagrada Familia is all mine. I strut about the scaffolding, high above Barcelona, basking in the warm glow of the setting sun, and breathing in every beautiful curl of stone.

You might wonder what on earth the builders have been doing for the last 120-odd years? Well, the strangeness of Gaudí's design meant that progress was slow while they got their heads around it and then in 1926, Gaudí sadly died, which further slowed things down – especially because he'd liked to make things up as he went along and no one was quite sure what he'd been planning. Then there's the fact that the costs of the building work have relied on donations, and people haven't always been willing to give money. Some because they weren't sure about Gaudí's design, others because they didn't trust the builders to do it justice.

Gaudí might have liked to change things as he went along, but he did *have* a plan and the current architects are doing their best to remain true to it. Thank goodness that enough people find delight and meaning in Sagrada Familia to want to make it a reality. I can't wait for the day that this amazing building is finished.

15

The Passion facade shows scenes from Christ's death. Sagrada has two other main facades. One is showing his birth and one is showing humans' journey towards God.

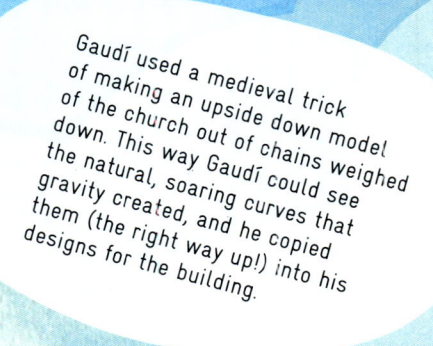

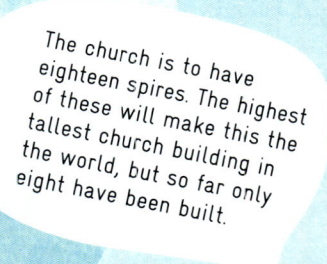

Gaudí used a medieval trick of making an upside down model of the church out of chains weighed down. This way Gaudí could see the natural, soaring curves that gravity created, and he copied them (the right way up!) into his designs for the building.

The church is to have eighteen spires. The highest of these will make this the tallest church building in the world, but so far only eight have been built.

16 THE FOREST OF DREAMS A.K.A BASILICA DE LA SAGRADA FAMILIA

Inside the church, the supporting columns branch out at the top, merging with the decorative ceiling as if they somehow grow into it.

THE WATERY WARREN
a.k.a Venice

> The stunning Rialto Bridge has rows of shops running its length on either side.

> The remarkable Ca d'Oro, or House of Gold, built in 1430, belonged to one of the wealthiest families in Venice. It was highly decorated with gold and other semi-precious metals, only some of which still remain.

> St Mark's Basilica is a very ornate church attached to the Doge's Palace. It was his private chapel until it became available for public use in 1807.

From Spain to Italy. Far below me, I spotted the rich, colourful tapestry of Venice, woven through with miles of canals, gleaming like hundreds of silvery threads in the afternoon sun. Venice, a city-state in Northern Italy, is heaven for pigeons – most of us make a pilgrimage here at some point in our lives, which might explain why there are usually more of us than there are humans in Piazza San Marco (St Mark's Square), the spectacular main open area in the heart of the city.

The reason, quite simply, is that this city is full of the most exquisite, medieval architecture in the world: there's no place like it on earth. Set in a lagoon (a huge 'lake' of sea water just near the ocean), the city is built on 118 small islands, connected by bridges – about 380 on my last count. Amongst these islands winds a labyrinth of canals, over which glide many gondolas – these are small boats, which are used here in the same way cars are on roads in nearly every other city in the world. I must say, it's a very pleasant change to not have to splutter through the usual haze of smog from car exhausts. As I wheeled across the blue sky, however, I did get a whiff

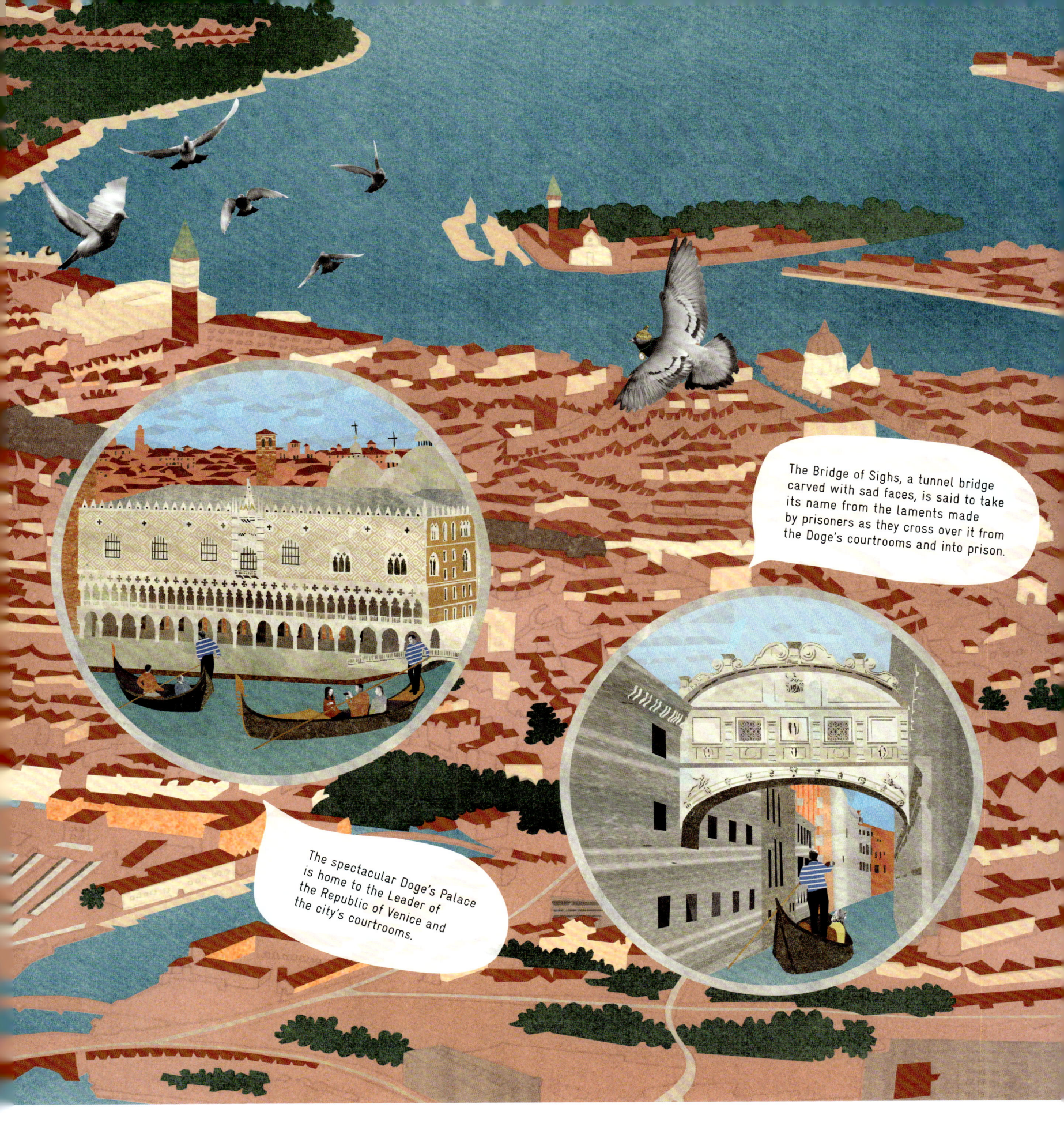

The Bridge of Sighs, a tunnel bridge carved with sad faces, is said to take its name from the laments made by prisoners as they cross over it from the Doge's courtrooms and into prison.

The spectacular Doge's Palace is home to the Leader of the Republic of Venice and the city's courtrooms.

of that unmistakeable Venetian pong: a mix of sea air and stagnant pond, always a lot stronger in warm weather. Flapping down towards St Mark's Square, I felt almost at home again. Everywhere I looked, crowds of pigeons pecked and strutted, flapped and cooed. At one point three boys chased into a crowd of us and as one, wings beating powerfully, we took off, flying around the square and swooping near their heads before perching on the belltower of St Mark's Basilica – what larks!

Nothing could mar my delight at being back in Venice again, and as I had another flap around later, I feasted my eyes on the fascinating tangle below: elegant, ornate buildings painted in deep, rich colours; passageways and courtyards; bridges and squares; churches, belltowers and statues, and water, water, everywhere ... really, Venice is like a fairytale legend that has risen from the deep and may one day return. That's not actually far from the truth – water and stone aren't the best of friends, and after centuries of being wet, many of its buildings are beginning to crumble. Get there as soon as you can!

19

THE FLOATING FANCY
a.k.a San Giorgio Maggiore

The bell tower is not actually attached to the church, but it is absolutely a part of San Giorgio Maggiore's famous silhouette when seen from across the water.

One very famous church in Venice is San Giorgio Maggiore, which sits across the water from St Mark's Square on the edge of a little island. I decided to visit it this morning and was just about to take off, when I heard a 'Yoo-hoo!' and turned to see my Auntie Waddleclaw! What a small world ... Auntie decided to join me, and together, we squinted out across the shining water to the church.

With its striking white marble front, San Giorgio Maggiore gleamed bright in the morning sun, and seemed almost to float above the dark channel of water beneath it. The church was completed in 1610 and designed by a famous Italian architect called Palladio, who made it fashionable to recreate the look of classical Greek temples. However, he had a conundrum when trying to fit this kind of front onto a traditional Christian church. Greek temples were essentially big, rectangular rooms, while churches usually follow the shape of a cross with one longer room called a nave and then a shorter one crossing it called the transept. To fit a classical, rectangular front onto this cross shape, Palladio had to merge two fronts (or 'facades'): one tall and thin and the other shorter and wider.

20 THE FLOATING FANCY A.K.A SAN GIORGIO MAGGIORE

> The architect, Palladio, said, 'Of all the colours, none is more proper for churches than white; since the purity of colour, as of the life, is particularly gratifying to God.'

> On calm days, the church's reflection shimmers just beneath it, like the ghostly church of another city submerged beneath the waters.

Somehow, he managed to make this mixed-up double-facade look magnificent – although from the air, we could see that the white marble is not carried through around the rest of the building, which is built in plain brown brick. Auntie thought it looked a bit, 'puffy breast but mangy tailed', but I pointed out that Palladio did this deliberately to make his facade look all the more splendid.

We couldn't actually get inside but we had a good old gander from one of the higher windowsills. There was a wonderful sense of brightness everywhere: the walls were painted in soft whites and greys, and on them danced those lovely ever-changing shimmers from light reflecting on water. The mood was solemn and peaceful and much of the church was quite plain – a soothing change from some churches which are so crammed with beautiful things that you almost feel a bit overwhelmed (Canterbury Cathedral, anyone?).

The calm didn't last long, though. As we gazed through the window, a deafening bong almost knocked us off our perch as the bell struck the hour. With an indignant squawk, Auntie leapt into the air and off we flapped, ears ringing, back out over the water.

MURDER RING
a.k.a Colosseum

It was extremely hot today and I must say I was starting to feel a bit roasted as I sailed into Rome, through a deep blue sky. But nothing could spoil the thrill I felt as I caught my first glimpse of the Colosseum, an ancient stadium built by the Romans over 2,000 years ago for their gladiator games.

It reminded me of a fancy wedding cake, albeit one that's been attacked by a hungry child. Parts of the Colosseum now stand in ruins because of its great age, but this is still an amazingly solid structure to have survived for so long. When it was built, the Romans had just created a new, stronger mix for concrete and that, along with some new discoveries in building techniques, meant they were able to build up and up, higher into our sky-realm than ever before.

The Colosseum has seen all kinds of use. It began life as an amphitheatre. But long after the people who had built it were dead and gone, the Colosseum continued to be useful to humans, just in different ways. Over the centuries, people lived in it, set up little workshops in it, used it as a fortress and at one time even used it as a Christian church and graveyard for the dead.

One of the oldest (and largest) amphitheatres in the world, the Colosseum was used for gladiatorial contests and public spectacles such as animal hunts, executions and theatrical dramas.

There are eighty exits leading out of the amphitheatre so there weren't too many queues to get out at home-time. These were called 'Vomitorium', which is where your human word 'vomit' comes from: food making a quick exit!

I perched high above the arena on the back of a seat, and looked around at the vast space stretching around me. Stunning. But I'm in two minds about the Colosseum. On the one wing, I love its colossal size and beauty, and how its very existence depended on teamwork and skill. And I love how it has managed to survive for so long, despite taking quite a battering from all its different uses across the centuries. But on the other wing, I can't believe what it was first built for and what went on in here! Coo! For five centuries, human beings cheered and clapped as they watched people hacking each other – as well as lions, tigers, even elephants – to pieces.

The sheer size of the Colosseum shows how popular those games were – it had 50,000 seats – as big as a modern stadium. I looked around and tried to imagine this enormous space when it was new and intact. A thick roar of bloodlusty excitement thunders out from the crowd, rolling high around the circular wall. I shivered, despite the hot sun. Funny creatures, you humans – such refined surroundings, and such brutality within.

23

All the 50,000 seats in the Colosseum had numbers – spectators were given little broken bits of pottery with a matching number on it so they could find their seat.

The 'hypogeum' was where the gladiators and animals were kept, in a warren of tunnels, cells and sophisticated gates. It also had a private passage for the Emperor and other important spectators to come and go – an ancient VIP entrance.

Sometimes the amphitheatre was flooded with water for displays by specially trained swimming animals such as bulls and horses, or the re-enactment of famous sea battles with real ships! Wow!

24 MURDER RING A.K.A COLOSSEUM

The amphitheatre was designed as a circle ringed with ties of elegant arches and columns.

In the first gladiatorial games ever held here, over 9,000 animals were killed in a matter of weeks.

BUILDING BRIDGES

A simple beam bridge

A truss bridge

A suspension bridge

Some of the most breathtaking moments on my trip have been when I spotted a monumental bridge soaring across the empty space of a valley, its natural curve echoing the bow of a rainbow or the hang of a spider's web. I've heard many humans speak of the amazing feeling of being suspended in the air when crossing a high bridge. Perhaps it gives you a glimpse of what it is like to fly?

I often wonder how some bridges stay up and manage to take the loads put upon them. While every bridge is different – built to meet the particular requirements of the space it needs to cross – there are various types of bridges. Let me give you a quick rundown:

I have been in the air for several weeks now, flying over towns and cities, vast stretches of open countryside, dark rivers, lonely temples and wild, silent mountains. I've had a lot of time to think about the buildings I have seen, and I must say, I lower my head to you humans, for I am struck by your species' remarkable ingenuity, skill and desire for progress. There is one architectural feature in particular that seems to sum this up: the bridge.

A BEAM BRIDGE

This is the simplest kind of bridge: one where the whole weight of anything crossing is taken by a single horizontal deck (the bit you walk/drive on), supported at each end. If a beam bridge needs to cross a wide distance, the deck needs more support, or it would begin to bend in the middle under a heavy load. In this case, it can be adapted into:

A TRUSS BRIDGE

To make a beam bridge stronger, the easiest thing to do is just make the beam thicker and stronger, but that can make the bridge heavy, expensive and hard to build. Instead, the best, most efficient support is called a 'truss', which is, quite simply, a triangle (or, usually, triangles). When triangles are lined up next to each other and connected, the resulting 'truss' is just as strong as a solid beam would be, but it uses much less material, resulting in a lighter, longer bridge.

A SUSPENSION BRIDGE

Here, the deck is supported from above. Very long cables are attached to the top of vertical towers. The cable is held down at the sides, where the bridge meets the earth, by heavy blocks called anchorages. The deck hangs from this long suspension cable with the help of shorter, vertical cables.

AN ARCH BRIDGE

An arch bridge is kind of like an upside-down suspension bridge. The deck sits on top the arch, which is held in place by its own weight. But as the weight pushes down, it also pushes out, so the arch needs heavy weights at either end to stop its ends spreading apart. These are a little like the anchorages in a suspension bridge, except they push in towards the bridge rather than pulling out away from it. So those are the basic types of bridges, but there is an endless variety of ways that these structures can be applied and mixed together. Now turn the page to see some of my absolute favourite bridges.

An arch bridge

GOLDEN GATE BRIDGE, USA

With its distinctive red colour, Golden Gate is a classic suspension bridge, built in 1937 to connect the city of San Francisco with Marin County. It crosses a vast distance of water, about as long as 400 Olympic-sized swimming pools laid end to end, and the forces that the bridge has to balance against are formidable: this body of water is right next to the ocean, so it is full of strong, swirling tides and currents; there are lots of strong winds; 100,000 cars cross the bridge every day, and there are even earthquakes from time to time! It's so high that its towers are often lost in the clouds and, from the footpath, the famous prison island of Alcatraz is visible, across the bay.

MILLAU VIADUCT, FRANCE

The tallest bridge in the world when it was finished in 2004, this viaduct was built in part to solve the problem of holiday traffic, as people drove down through France to Spain. The view is so spectacular that people often slow down as they drive over the bridge to take photographs, and the speed limit had to be lowered! Although it looks a little like a suspension bridge, the Millau Viaduct is actually a 'cable-stayed' bridge: the deck is supported both from below, by giant piers, and from above, by cables. The winds at the top of this massive structure are too strong for a bird like me to perch there – I prefer viewing this magnificent bridge from the safety of the hills, while nibbling on a leftover morsel of baguette from a pique-nique …

Golden Gate Bridge, USA

Millau Viaduct, France

TOWER BRIDGE, UK

Finished in 1894, Tower Bridge stands over the busy River Thames, once a trading passage to London's docks for ships from all over the world. It is a suspension bridge, but because it needed to be designed so that all sizes of boat could pass beneath it, its architects created a 'bascule' section in the middle, a fancy name for a drawbridge that can be raised in two halves to allow tall ships to pass under.

Tower Bridge is my favourite bridge in the world – my dear Elsie and I were betrothed on its walkway, many years ago.

BROOKLYN BRIDGE, USA

Completed in 1883, Brooklyn Bridge was the first steel-wire suspension bridge, and the longest of its kind when it was built. Its architect, John Roebling, suffered an injury while surveying the site from which he died soon after, but not before ensuring that his design could take six times the load it needed to, meaning that the bridge has lasted this long and been able to adapt to all sorts of different kinds of traffic. Some of its strength is because it has both vertical cables, like the Golden Gate, and diagonal cables, like the Millau Viaduct, and they criss-cross to make a beautiful pattern, like a web of diamonds. In my humble opinion, there is no better spot from which to gaze at the fabulous glittering New York skyline.

THE MYSTERIOUS MATHEMATICAL MIRACLE

a.k.a. Great Pyramid of Giza

The height of the Great Pyramid is 146.5 metres – that's taller than ten buses balanced end to end on top of one another!

The pyramids are perfect geometrical triangles and the sides of the Great Pyramid precisely face the four points of the compass. It's still a mystery just how the ancient Egyptians achieved such accurate measurements without the help of calculators and computers.

The pyramids have always fascinated me, surrounded with their tales of myth and mystery. Built by the Egyptians nearly 5,000 years ago as tombs for their Pharaohs (Kings), there are over 130 remaining. Of these, the Great Pyramid of Giza is the biggest and most splendid: built for the mummy of the Pharaoh Khufu, it is the last of the Seven Ancient Wonders of the World still left standing.

I had to take several rests as I flapped my way slowly from the capital city of Cairo out into the hot desert. At one point, I hitched a ride on the back of a camel, but as soon as I spotted the Great Pyramid through the shimmering heat haze, I took to the air once more, my heart pounding with excitement. And then, I did it: I landed on the Great Pyramid of Giza. Incredible! My claws were actually touching stones carefully placed by builders thousands years ago!

Originally, the pyramid was covered by an outer casing of smooth white stone, which must have looked magnificent, gleaming bright in the African sun. These outer stones were loosened by a huge earthquake in the fourteenth century and were carted away to be used for other buildings! Not very respectful,

Standing near the Great Pyramid is the Sphinx – a huge, impressive statue of the Pharaoh with a lion's body.

The Great Pyramid is surrounded by several smaller ones for Pharaoh Khufu's wives and family.

eh? And that's not all that was taken. Like most graves, the pyramid was sealed after the Pharoah's body was placed inside, surrounded by a wealth of treasures to see him through to the next world. But over the centuries, robbers broke in and stole everything. Charming!

One of the many mysteries surrounding the pyramids is just *how* they were built. For instance, the huge stones that make up the Great Pyramid weigh several tonnes each and are thought to have been transported from over 800 kilometres away. And there are 2.3 *million* blocks like these. Now I don't know about you, but I'm thinking that, in a time before machinery, that's a *lot* of hard work for the builders. How did they manage it!? Most experts agree that the stones were probably brought on boats along the Nile river before being pulled up to the pyramid on a system of ramps and pulleys.

You humans today think you're so advanced, but when you think about how much the Egyptians obviously knew – not to mention discover that pigeons are actually architecture experts – does it make you wonder whether there might be other stuff you haven't figured out … ?

THE PALACE OF GHOSTS
a.k.a Taj Mahal

The four minarets – towers from which Muslims are called to prayer – are each built to lean slightly away from the dome. According to some specialists, this is part of the original design so that they do not damage the dome if they should ever fall.

The platform is the size of eight Olympic-size pools.

Pigeons know what love is. When a pigeon finds a mate, we stay together for life. So I understand how Emperor Shah Jahan must have felt when his wife, Mumtaz Mahal, died young. He had loved her dearly and, as a way of showing his grief, he built her a monument so magnificent that it would be spoken of all around the world for centuries to come. I once pecked a heart in the trunk of an oak tree for Elsie ... but it's not quite the same thing, I grant you.

I flew in to Agra, in India, early this morning, flapping unhurriedly over the wide Yamuna river, taking in the unfamiliar sights and smells. Mist hung in places above the water, but the sun was already warm on my back. Then, suddenly, there it stood before me, gleaming in the dawn light and almost seeming to hover over its own perfect reflection below. The Taj Mahal. Wowza.

I swooped down and skimmed low and fast along the length of the ornamental pool leading up to the mausoleum; once again the Taj's mirror image lay beneath me in the still water. Fluttering up, I got a perch high atop the enormous dome (and I'm talking E. Nor. Mous: about as tall as eight

Legend has it that when the Taj was completed, Shah Jahan chopped off the hands of all the workers who had helped build it, so they would never again be able to create anything so beautiful.

double-decker buses stacked on top of each other) for a good look around.

Breathtaking. The Taj Mahal is like something straight out of a fairy tale – a fantasy building. Everywhere you look there is beauty. Arabic words from the Qur'an, the Muslim holy book, dance on the walls, inlaid in black and white marble. Elsewhere walls are decorated with delicate flowers, or carved into screens of intricate patterns, that filter the sun's strong, bright light. Arches and slender minarets raise your gaze to the heavens, while within lie the skeletons of Mumtaz and Shah Jahan himself, who was buried beside her when he died in 1666.

I spent an entire day here marvelling at the Taj's beauty, relatively undisturbed (except for one little incident with a very rude tour guide that I won't set down here). Almost before I knew it, dusk was falling. I glided back towards the nearby city of Agra, thinking of how everything about this building speaks of Shah Jahan's love: for his wife, his religion and for beauty. I think the Taj Mahal is probably as close to paradise as it's possible to get on this earth. Sigh.

The massive dome is known as an onion or guava dome because of its shape.

The garden was originally laid out to look like Paradise as described in the Qur'an, the Muslim holly book: filled with abundant trees, flowers, plants and birds.

The Mughal Emperors were great pigeon fanciers, y'know – Shah Jahan's father, Akbar the Great, took 2,000 birds with him wherever he travelled.

34 THE PALACE OF GHOSTS A.K.A TAJ MAHAL

Mumtaz's tomb is placed exactly at the centre of the building – everything outwards of this is symmetrical, except for Shah Jahan's tomb, which was placed next to Mumtaz's when he died (and rather spoils the whole effect, if you ask me!).

The Taj was described as 'a teardrop on the cheek of eternity' by Rabindranath Tagore, poet and philosopher.

Taj Mahal's translucent white marble walls are inlaid with countless precious stones, inside and out: jade, turquoise, sapphire ... twenty-eight different kinds, carried from all over Asia by an army of 1,000 elephants.

THE GREAT WORM
a.k.a Great Wall of China

> The wall travels along almost half of China, twisting this way and that, over mountains, across grasslands, through desert and on and on, for 21 *thousand* kilometres!

Elsie once told me she'd read in a newspaper that the Great Wall of China can be seen from space! I'm not sure that can really be true, but it gives some idea about the sheer size of this structure. As I approached, I have to admit I flew as high as possible, just to try to get up far enough to see the whole thing from end to end – but all I did was make myself dizzy. The truth is, it's impossible to see all of it at once.

The Great Wall is actually a collection of lots of different walls, built over 2,000 years at different times, in different styles, out of different materials and for different purposes. Different-ola! In some places it doesn't even join together! But these different sections do have a shared story to tell, and that is about human beings' (very peculiar) desire to OWN things.

The oldest parts of the wall were built in around 700 BC as barricades, put up by local landowners to protect their patch from invading neighbours. Mine, mine, mine! In those days, the wall would have been made simply by forcing wooden boards into the ground. Then, around 200 BC, the First Emperor of China conquered all these landowners and ordered that their individual

Watchtowers were built along the wall where supplies and weapons could be stored, soldiers could sleep or shelter, and from which fire or smoke signals could be sent to other watchtowers further along the wall, as a way of passing on messages.

Battlements provided protection from attack.

At one particularly steep section of the wall, near a hilltop village called Mutianyu, there's a slide set into the mountainside for visitors to whoosh down after they've climbed up to the top! Woo hoo!

walls be joined together and made into one single wall, marking out *his* new Empire. This new wall travelled a long way through China, and each section was built by local builders, who used whatever materials were available nearby: stones in the mountains or tightly packed mud on the plains.

It wasn't until the powerful Emperors of the Ming dynasty came along in the fourteenth century that the Great Wall as we know it today began.

By then, they mostly built it out of bricks and a glue (or 'mortar') made of sticky rice and limestone. I bet *those* workers never went hungry! Battlements and watchtowers were built for defending the Empire, as well as ensuring that no one got in or out without paying tax to the Emperor's officials posted along its length. Mine, mine, mine: again.

The Great Wall is a unique structure. It is almost a living thing – for centuries it's been wriggling its way across the land and telling its stories about human power, aggression and greed. Still – I s'pose there's a lot of architecture that might not exist if it weren't for those human traits.

37

THE LITTLE GREY BOX
a.k.a Church of the Light

> The walls are so thick and solid that when you walk in, it feels like somebody has turned down the volume.

> The cross in the wall is the only religious symbol in the whole room. It allows natural light into the church.

To be perfectly honest, I wasn't overly excited about visiting this Japanese church. Generally, I like grand, dramatic buildings that thrill you with their sheer size or stunning decoration. From what I'd heard, this sounded like a plain grey concrete block, sitting amongst ordinary houses in an ordinary neighbourhood – all so ordinary, in fact, that you could almost miss it.

Which is precisely what I did this morning, and I admit I was muttering a little to myself as I coasted around the suburbs of the city of Ibaraki, trying to find the peckin' thing. Finally I spotted it and fluttered down towards the flat grey roof. Hm. So far, so unremarkable. Unfortunately, the same couldn't be said for my landing, which was less than dignified, as I slipped and slithered about on the unexpectedly smooth surface. This concrete was nothing like your usual carpark stuff. In fact, up close, I noticed that it was rather glossy and beautiful, with soft, translucent greys that reminded me of Elsie's downy wing feathers. Apparently, this very special, dense kind of concrete had been carefully created by the architect, Tadao Ando, and his team of experts. Once

38 THE LITTLE GREY BOX A.K.A CHURCH OF THE LIGHT

Visitors enter the church through its angled entrance.

it was mixed, they followed the usual process of pouring the liquid concrete into specially built wooden frames called 'formwork'. But when the concrete had hardened, the frames were carefully removed and reused to build the simple benches and pews for the congregation to sit on, instead of being thrown away.

I sidled in through the angled entrance and came into what felt like another world.

It was so quiet! I could no longer hear a plane high above, or cars passing in the street. Suddenly it was just me and the space I stood in. And in that space, I was aware of two things: darkness and light. The dark was around me in the plain grey concrete walls and simple wooden benches. And the light – the light! Piercing the gloom, an impossibly bright cross cut across the far wall. Through it streamed the morning sunlight, filling that plain little church with golden rays of glory. It was absolutely breathtaking!

Far from boring and ordinary, I've decided this church is thrilling and *extra*ordinary. It may be simple, and made from a plain, inexpensive and humble material, but that only serves to make its other main material all the more glorious: universal, eternal *light*.

39

HUNGRY BEAKS HALL
a.k.a Sydney Opera House

In the concert halls, Utzon thought carefully about the acoustics – the way sound travels around a room. He panelled the walls and ceiling with overlapping plywood sheets, so that the soundwaves cascaded along them. Music travels and still sounds beautiful to the people sitting at the back.

Utzon and his team used a very early computer to work out the best way of constructing the shells so that they looked great and – more importantly! – didn't collapse.

Everybody knows the Sydney Opera House; it's one of the most famous buildings in the world and pops up on TV at the merest mention of Australia. If you haven't seen it before, then you really ought to watch more television. But I couldn't wait to see it with my own eyes. I approached Sydney after a long-haul flight over the Pacific ocean, and the Opera House made a truly impressive sight as I coasted in across the harbour; those great white crests rearing up over the water, like enormous shells washed up by the sea, or the billowing sails of a giant ship. They remind me of hungry baby beaks, eager for food – but that's probably just a pigeon thing.

Tired though I was, I couldn't resist swooping low and skimming just above the gleaming smooth curves of the roofs. Up close, you can see that they are armour-plated with thousands of white and cream tiles that sparkle and glisten in the sunshine. I didn't fancy a skid landing on those, so I fluttered down onto the forecourt. All around me people were enjoying themselves: strolling, chatting, eating ice cream or sitting on the wide steps leading down to the street.

The Opera House is built on a platform that also makes a lovely big public space that anyone can use – even pigeons!

Before long, a tour guide began her talk and I sidled up to eavesdrop.

She said that the Sydney Opera House was designed by Danish architect Jørn Utzon as a centre for the arts – not only opera but also ballet, theatre and concerts. It has restaurants, cafés, bars and shops – coo! Chuck in a couple of bedrooms and you'd never have to leave!

Unfortunately, not all of the Opera House quite went to plan. Like Gaudí (see Basilica de la Sagrada Familia, pages 14–17), Utzon was an architect who changed his designs as he went along. While the Opera House was still being constructed, he had a disagreement with the Sydney government. Utzon felt they were spoiling his ideas by wanting everything to be cheaper and finally became so frustrated that he walked out, never to return. The Opera House was completed in 1973 without him, but perhaps not quite in the way he would have liked. A shame, but there you go – some days you're the pigeon, some days you're the statue. It doesn't change the fact that he designed a truly magnificent piece of architecture.

THE BIG BIRD
a.k.a. Brasilia

To get the city done in time, building work went on day and night, non-stop for four years, and employed over 60,000 construction workers.

Like Venice (see pages 18-19), Brasilia (pronounced Brazi-ya, if you want to sound like you've been there) is a must-see for pigeons, though you could not find two cities more different.

Brasilia is the capital of Brazil in South America. It was built to take over from the old capital, Rio de Janeiro, which sits on Brazil's east coast, because it was decided that the capital city should be more in the centre of such a huge country.

And so began the careful planning that went into every element of Brasilia. Unlike most cities, which grow and develop over hundreds of years, Brasilia is only about as old as your grandad: it was built in just four years between 1956 and 1960! The famous architect Oscar Niemeyer was appointed head architect in charge of designing all the public buildings of the city – what a challenge!

Since I arrived here a couple of days ago, I've found it extremely easy to find my way around from the air – although some visitors on foot complain that because everywhere looks so similar, it's also easy to get lost.

Flying from above, you can see the city has been designed to look like a plane or a bird with outstretched wings.

Streets here were designed with car travel in mind, and they criss-cross one another through numbered blocks – each address has a number, rather than a street or neighbourhood name.

In fact, maybe the layout of the city works best from a bird's eye view. The main government buildings are placed in the 'head' or 'cockpit', while other kinds of buildings are grouped elsewhere: there's a hotel sector, a banking sector and so on. The areas where people live were carefully planned to have a mix of luxurious and affordable housing, as well as different sorts of schools, shops, and open spaces like parks.

Brasilia was an architect's dream: to be able to apply ideas about architecture to a whole city at once was something that had never been attempted on this scale before – although every so often over the centuries, planners have tried to make a clean sweep of the higgledy-piggledy centres of older cities that have sprouted up over time in a more haphazard way. It's a great place for an architecture fan, full of exciting buildings that explore new, unusual structures and forms. Turn the page for a taster!

43

The Cathedral of Brasilia is such a dramatic building! Every element of it looks energetic, gathering itself like a volcano erupting skywards – or perhaps it is a sunflower, face upturned, or maybe hands reaching towards the heavens.

The National Congress complex looks like a space station on the moon. The Secretariat (the double-vertical building) stands between the Chamber of Deputies and the Senate (the two curving dishes, one facing up, the other down).

The largest buildings in the city, they are deeply symbolic, designed to convey importance, seriousness and power.

THE BIG BIRD A.K.A. BRASILIA

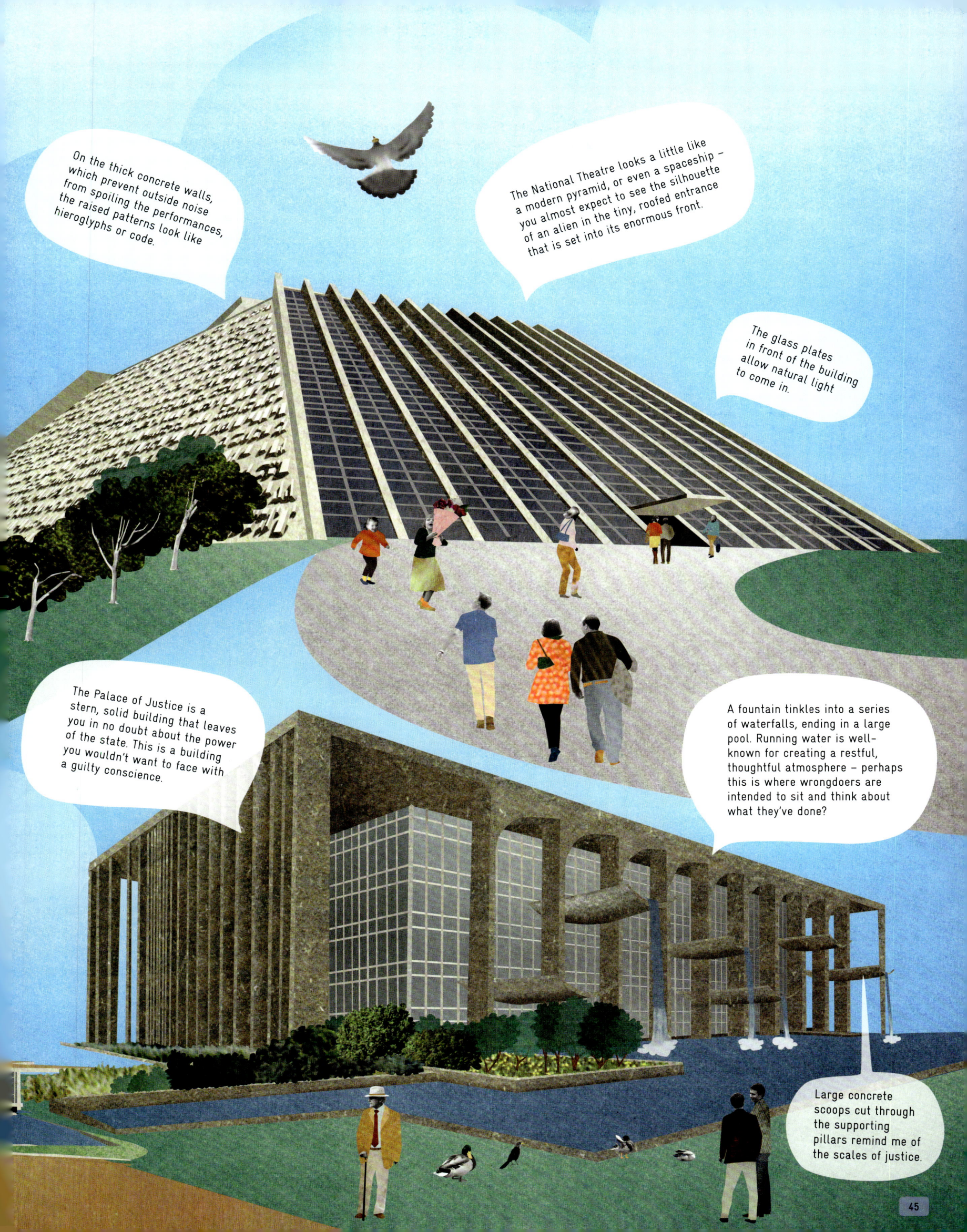

On the thick concrete walls, which prevent outside noise from spoiling the performances, the raised patterns look like hieroglyphs or code.

The National Theatre looks a little like a modern pyramid, or even a spaceship – you almost expect to see the silhouette of an alien in the tiny, roofed entrance that is set into its enormous front.

The glass plates in front of the building allow natural light to come in.

The Palace of Justice is a stern, solid building that leaves you in no doubt about the power of the state. This is a building you wouldn't want to face with a guilty conscience.

A fountain tinkles into a series of waterfalls, ending in a large pool. Running water is well-known for creating a restful, thoughtful atmosphere – perhaps this is where wrongdoers are intended to sit and think about what they've done?

Large concrete scoops cut through the supporting pillars remind me of the scales of justice.

45

MY BEST TOWERS EVER

I'm a big fan of towers: the thing about them is ... well ... they're high! That's really rather the point of them. The question is, why? Why go high rather than low? Why not make a building that travels along the ground for miles? Well, buster, you're asking the right pigeon. I'll tell you exactly what's with all the *up*ness. The taller you are, the more powerful you seem. If you're high up, you can also see further and spot an enemy approaching from afar. Humans have always known this ... so they have built towers to make them feel safe and secure: castles and fortresses, beacons and lighthouses. Plus the views are fantastic. THAT's what's with all the upness.

There's just one leetle problem with towers: getting up to the top. Easy peasy for pigeons, less so for you chaps. I feel for you, I really do – just looking at some of those winding staircases makes me feel out of puff. And over the centuries, with new discoveries in building techniques and materials, towers have reached new heights, meaning more ... pant ... wheeze ... stairs.

Shanghai World Financial Center, China. 492 metres

Eiffel Tower, France. 324 metres

Agbar Tower, Spain. 144 metres

Television Tower, Germany. 368 metres

Turning Torso, Sweden. 190 metres

Big Ben, UK. 98 metres

Petronas Towers, Malaysia. 452 metres

Then came a development towards the end of the nineteenth century, which meant not only that towers could be built higher than ever before, but – thank goodness! – solved the stair problem at the same time. It became possible to make a super-strong material called steel in large, affordable quantities. Steel was so strong and yet relatively light enough that it could be used to support really enormous towers. Steel cables were also strong enough to support elevators to get up to the top – bye bye stairs.

Just in time, because a new reason for building towers was developing: space, or rather, the lack of it. By this time, more and more people were living in cities – so many people, in fact, that there wasn't room for them all. In the middle of a city there isn't much space for new buildings to spread out, but there is always space to build up. And so the twentieth century saw bigger and bolder towers than ever before, filled with everything from homes and offices to swimming pools, helipads, small golf courses, gyms, ballrooms, hospitals and rotating restaurants! And the twenty-first century is seeing even more amazing towers – ones that twist and taper and – ooh, I've seen some corkers on my travels! Look at these lovelies…

Empire State Building, USA. 381 metres

Transamerica Pyramid, USA. 260 metres

Moscow State University, Russia. 240 metres

Burj Khalifa, Dubai. 828 metres

SEAGRAM BUILDING, NEW YORK CITY, USA

This skyscraper was built in 1958 and designed by the famous architect Mies van der Rohe. He believed that the skeleton of a building should be echoed on its outside and that would make it look beautiful without any other decoration. And so we can see beams – smaller versions of the steel skeleton that hold the whole building up – on the outside and inbetween the 'skin' of big glass panels fitted as windows.

CHINA CENTRAL TELEVISION (CCTV) HEADQUARTERS, BEIJING, CHINA

To me, this is one of the most extraordinary buildings in the world. Completed in 2008, the design makes a giant – and very unusual – loop! To make this looping tower shape possible, the steel skeleton has been arranged in diamonds which have different sizes depending on the work they have to do and the weight they have to support. Since the tower is built in an area known for possible earthquakes, even if the ground shifts, the building won't collapse. Pretty amazing for a building known to the locals as 'Big Boxer Shorts' because of its funny shape … !

LEANING TOWER OF PISA, ITALY

This round bell tower was planned to be the tallest in Italy when it was begun in 1173. During the first stage of building, the bottom three floors suddenly tilted and sank into the ground because the foundations weren't strong enough to support the tower's weight! The tower was finally completed in 1360, although it's never been made to stand straight.

Seagram Building, USA. 157 metres

Leaning Tower of Pisa, Italy. 54 metres

LONDON BRIDGE TOWER (OR 'THE SHARD'), LONDON, ENGLAND

The tallest tower in Europe when it was completed in 2012, this steel-framed, glass panelled skyscraper contains offices, a hotel, luxury homes, shops, restaurants and a spa. It was designed by Renzo Piano, who described it as 'almost like a kaleidoscope, a mirror of London', and its pyramid shape is intended as a modern answer to the many church spires in the city.

CCTV Headquarters, China. 234 metres

London Bridge Tower, England. 308 metres

FALLINGWATER

a.k.a Fallingwater – our pigeon name for the building is the same!

Fallingwater was built as a holiday home for a rich family, who asked architect Frank Lloyd Wright to design a house for a particular spot in the woods that they loved, near a magnificent waterfall.

Most of Fallingwater is built from the same sandstone rock that the waterfall flows over, taken from a place further upstream.

I've been staying in Pittsburgh, USA, for a couple of days, visiting old friends and resting after my long fly from Brazil, which left me a little tired. But today I felt full of anticipation as I winged off on the two-hour trip to Bear Run, where Fallingwater stands, surrounded by glorious woodland. As I glided, I noticed autumn has caught up with me – there was a cold tang in the air, despite the warm sunshine, and the leaves of the trees were turning glorious reds and oranges. From what I'd heard, this house was really going to waft my wings. I love nature. I love architecture. In nearly all of his buildings, Frank Lloyd Wright, the architect, was interested in putting the two together: exploring the relationship between humans and nature, and blending indoor spaces with the outdoors. My first thoughts were that he did a flappin' good job, since it took me a while to even find Fallingwater!

The family who asked Wright to design this holiday home had been surprised when they understood what he was planning. They were expecting a house with a wonderful view of the waterfall. But instead he made the house *part* of the waterfall, with balconies

50 FALLINGWATER A.K.A FALLINGWATER

Steps lead from the sitting room directly down to the stream below.

staggered above it, like rock ledges. When I finally landed, the sound was so loud I could feel it thundering right up through my claws!

Everywhere I went, house and waterfall mingled together. Rushing noise could be heard from every part of the house. A rocky ledge of the waterfall jutted right up into the main sitting room and, in one passageway, water actually came inside and was channelled out again!

Visitors without wings need to cross a small bridge over the stream to reach the front door, and there they find a foot bath, which is also filled with water from the stream, for cleaning muddy boots. I took a quick drink and a wash in it and, feeling thoroughly refreshed, slowly flapped back towards the city and dinner, thinking about Fallingwater. It's a fabulous place – so unique and exciting. But one thing struck me – the whole house is made up of straight lines, something almost never seen in nature. To truly blend with its surroundings, should Wright have made Fallingwater look somehow rockier and craggier? But then would it have been so stylish? I'm not sure …

Frank Lloyd Wright designed the whole house, inside and out, including the furniture, to make sure everything fitted perfectly together.

Unwaxed slabs of the same stone as used on the floors rise around the huge stone fireplace in the sitting room, like dry rocks rising out of the water.

52 FALLINGWATER A.K.A FALLINGWATER

Frank Lloyd Wright designed these ingenious corner windows, so that every angle of the view is visible from inside the house.

On the floors the rock has been waxed, giving it a wet appearance.

53

KING OF THE CASTLES
a.k.a Chrysler Building

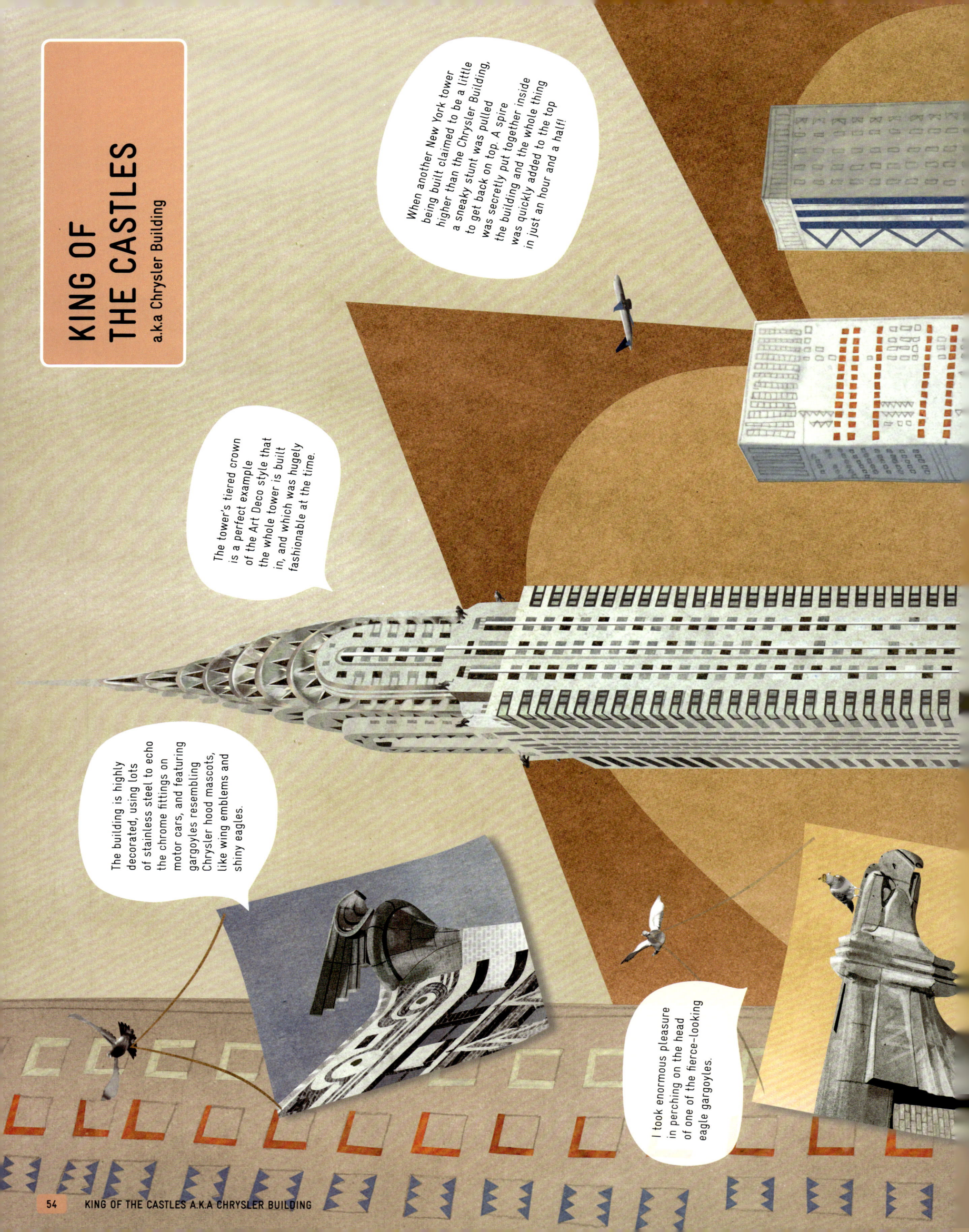

When another New York tower being built claimed to be a little higher than the Chrysler Building, a sneaky stunt was pulled to get back on top. A spire was secretly put together inside the building and the whole thing was quickly added to the top in just an hour and a half!

The tower's tiered crown is a perfect example of the Art Deco style that the whole tower is built in, and which was hugely fashionable at the time.

The building is highly decorated, using lots of stainless steel to echo the chrome fittings on motor cars, and featuring gargoyles resembling Chrysler hood mascots, like wing emblems and shiny eagles.

I took enormous pleasure in perching on the head of one of the fierce-looking eagle gargoyles.

54 KING OF THE CASTLES A.K.A CHRYSLER BUILDING

New York, New York ... every time I sail above this fabulous city, I get a shiver of pleasure at the thrilling bustle of life here. Far below, on the streets, people hurry past one another, and up above the buildings do the same: new jostling for space amongst the old, all thrusting ever higher to keep their place in the crowd.

A little bird once told me that New York was one of the fastest-growing cities in the twentieth century. Everywhere, everyone was clamouring to get a foothold and make something of themselves, and all this industry and buzz produced some very rich people, as well as some of the biggest, most spectacular – and most competitive – buildings in the world.

Step in, William P Chrysler: head of the Chrysler company, manufacturers of big, bold cars for big, bold owners. It was 1928 and he wanted to build a tower right in the centre of New York as headquarters for his company, as a display of his wealth, power and excellent taste, but also as a kind of gift to the city. He employed architect William Van Alen to create the most spectacular, the most impressive and, most importantly (to him), the tallest tower – not only in New York or America but ... (deep voice) the *world*.

Built using the very latest technology and architectural know-how, the Chrysler Building has a steel frame and brick 'skin'. When it was built, it was considered to be a city within a city – it had restaurants, stores, a beauty parlour, gyms and even a hospital! At the top, there was a private 'Cloud Club': a lounge and observation area.

Because of its decorative style, the tower came in for some criticism at first. There were those who thought that it was over-the-top, that there was something a bit flash and gaudy about it. Others worried that it was so very fashionable and 'of its time' that it would quickly go out of style. But rather than becoming outdated, the Chrysler Building has stood the test of time, becoming a much-loved part of the New York skyline, a monument to the era in which it was built and to the city itself.

> The tower was built in record time, with four floors going up a *week*.

55

THE SILVER SQUIGGLE
a.k.a Walt Disney Concert Hall

The outside is largely made up of panels of titanium, a silvery metal, which have been bent so they catch the light in different ways.

When it was first built, sunlight reflecting off the metal panels shone directly into people's homes nearby and blinded passing drivers. This problem was solved by sanding down the offending panels to make their surface less reflective.

I know, I know – the name Disney instantly makes you think of gloriously technicolour cartoons, but this building has nothing to do with the silver screen, rather with *music*: it is home to the Los Angeles Philharmonic Orchestra.

Soaring past the famous Hollywood sign and through the Los Angeles haze of late-afternoon sunshine, I spotted the concert hall shimmering below like a giant jewel. Fluffing feathers! It looked so effortless; so light and graceful, as if someone has drawn a floaty freehand fancy for the sheer fun of it. You would never know how heavy the materials used to build it are, and how carefully it had to be planned and engineered so that the whole thing could come together. In fact, this building couldn't have been designed at all without using a computer to calculate how the random-looking curves and wiggles would stand up. Fluttering past the bright metal curves of the building – I'd never get a foothold there; not a straight ledge or windowsill to be seen – I landed in the concert hall's charming gardens for a strut about. Someone had left an information leaflet on a nearby table and I hopped over for a quick read.

In the central auditorium, seating is arranged around the stage on all four sides, so everyone gets a view, and at the back of the hall sprout the unusual and dramatic-looking pipes of the organ, also designed by Gehry.

Gehry said that working with a computer on this building was like talking with 'a craftsman that understands me' – high praise for a box full of wires!

I knew that one of the most important things about any concert hall is the acoustics: the music needs to travel from each voice or instrument on the stage and reach everybody in the audience at the same time, sounding as good as it possibly can. Sound travels slowly – I'm sure you've seen a firework explode in the distance and heard the bang a second or two later – so this is a challenge for any architect. But Frank Gehry had it covered. The leaflet also described how, in this building, the main auditorium sits snug in the centre of the building, sealed off from outside noise. In fact, Gehry's design was so perfect that, for the first time, it was noticed that some notes on music sheets that had been owned by the orchestra for years were printed wrongly – no one had ever been able to hear that before! In this city of straight lined grids and low-level buildings, it filled me with delight to spot the bright, curvaceous wiggles of the concert hall. I love that such a serious building can look so completely bonkers - it actually *could* be something out of a cartoon! P'raps Gehry channelled a bit of the old Walt Disney spirit after all …

57

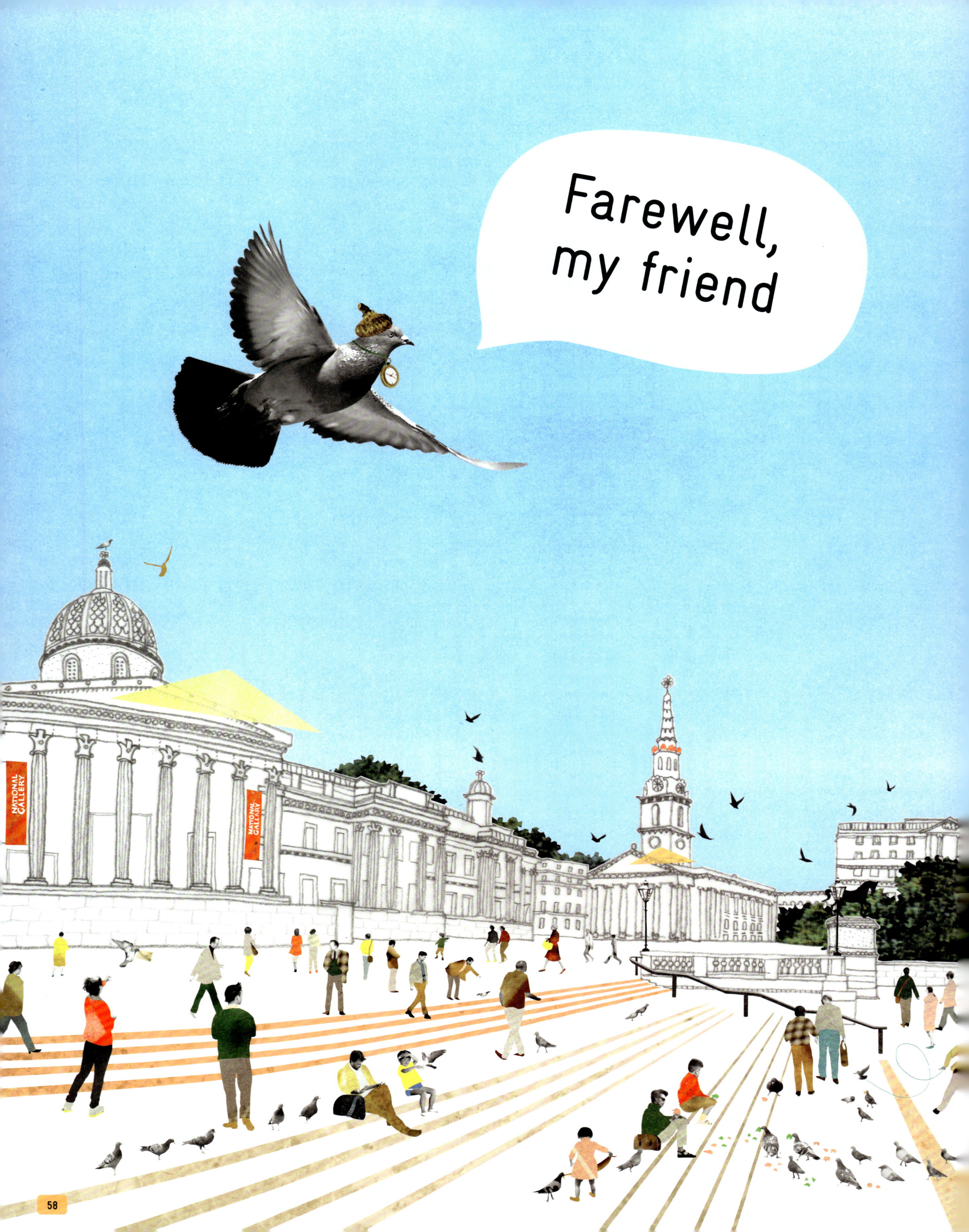
Farewell, my friend
NATIONAL GALLERY
NATIONAL GALLERY

What? Already?

I'm afraid so. It would seem our journey has come to an end. It is time for me to leave you and return to the open wings of my loving Elsie.

I do hope you have enjoyed our time together – I certainly have. We've visited some of the most thrilling and splendid buildings in the world, you and I, but there are still so many more out there for you to discover and explore.

If you take just one thing from this book, let it be this: the knowledge that architecture is about *you*; buildings are there for *you* to use and look at, and what *you* think of them is important.

What you think of pigeons is important too, of course. I very much hope that might have changed a little since we first met. Next time you see a pigeon – take a closer look and give it a wink – you might well get a knowing look and a cock of the head in return. I don't always wear my hat, y'know …

CANTERBURY CATHEDRAL
Canterbury, Kent, UK, Pages 6–7

Saint Augustine originally founded this cathedral in 597. In 1067, it was destroyed in a big fire and around 1070 a new building was commissioned by William the Conqueror, who was King of England from 1066 until his death in 1087. He was the only English king who couldn't speak English!

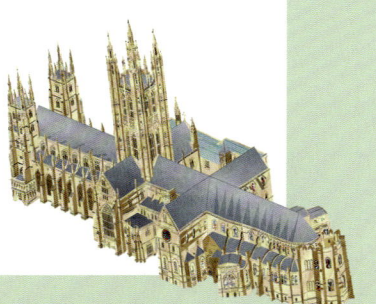

EIFFEL TOWER
Paris, France, Pages 8–9,

Gustave Eiffel was born in Dijon, France (where the mustard comes from!), in 1832. He built hundreds of metal structures all around the world, including the framework for the Statue of Liberty in New York City. He particularly loved to build railway bridges. He died in Paris in 1923.

GEORGES POMPIDOU CENTRE
Paris, France, Pages 10–11

The architects of the Pompidou Centre were both born in Italy: Renzo Piano in 1937 and Richard Rogers in 1933. Piano, who still lives in Italy, loves sailing and built his first boat at the age of eighteen. Rogers, whose official name is Baron Rogers of Riverside, lives and works in London.

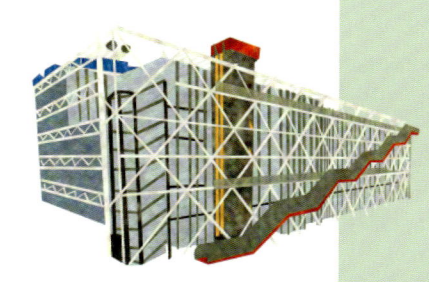

NOTRE-DAME DE RONCHAMP
near Mulhouse, France, Pages 12–13

Le Corbusier, whose real name was Charles-Edouard Jeanneret, was born in La Chaux-de-Fonds, Switzerland, in 1887. In 1920 he started calling himself Le Corbusier, as he wanted to have a name that people would remember. He died while swimming in the sea in the south of France, in 1965.

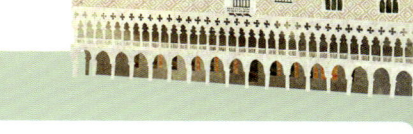

BASILICA DE LA SAGRADA FAMILIA
Barcelona, Spain, Pages 14–17

Antoni Gaudí was born in the region of Catalonia, Spain, in 1852. His first project was to design lampposts for one of Barcelona's squares and he went on to design many highly unusual buildings for the city, as well as the weird and wonderful Park Güell. He died in 1926.

CA D'ORO
Venice, Italy, Page 18

The Ca d'Oro (which means House of Gold) was built for the wealthy Contarini family in 1430. It now houses an art museum. It was built by a father and his son: Giovanni Bon (1355–1443) and Bartolomeo Bon (worked between 1421 and 1464) who were both architects and sculptors.

ST MARK'S BASILICA
Venice, Italy, Page 18

A basilica has stood here since 830 to house the relics (bones) of Saint Mark. The current church was commissioned around 1050 by Domenico Contarini, who ruled Venice between 1043 and 1071. It was a private chapel until 1807, when it became Venice's Roman Catholic cathedral.

RIALTO BRIDGE
Venice, Italy, Page 18

The Rialto Bridge is a bridge across the Grand Canal. It was completed in 1592 by Antonio da Ponte (1512–95) who is thought to have been born in Switzerland and whose surname, funnily enough, means 'bridge' in Italian! The present bridge is about the sixth version and the first to be built in stone - marble, in fact. The earlier bridges were made of wood.

DOGE'S PALACE
Venice, Italy, Page 19

First built in the twelfth century, the Doge's Palace was destroyed by a fire in 1577 but was later rebuilt. It was the residence of the Doge (the leaders of the Republic of Venice) as well as the seat of government, the law courts and the prison. It was rebuilt by Antonio da Ponte, who also built the Rialto Bridge.

BRIDGE OF SIGHS
Venice, Italy, Page 19

A tunnel bridge connecting the Doge's Palace with the prisons, the Bridge of Sighs was completed in about 1600. Antonio Contino was the nephew of Antonio da Ponte (who built the Rialto Bridge). It is not known exactly when he was born and died.

LEARN MORE ABOUT EACH BUILDING AND ITS ARCHITECT

SAN GIORGIO MAGGIORE
Venice, Italy, Pages 20–21

Andrea Palladio was born in Padua in 1508. He died in 1580 not far from Venice. He is considered one of the godfathers of modern architecture. Palladio's buildings were inspired by his studies of ancient Greek and Roman architecture. He is most famous for the many villas he built near Venice.

COLOSSEUM
Rome, Italy, Pages 22–25

The building of the Colosseum was ordered by Emperor Vespasian, who was born near Rome in the year 9 and who died in the year 79. Before he became Emperor, he commanded one of the four legions (a military unit of about 5,000 men) that invaded Britain in the year 43.

GOLDEN GATE BRIDGE
San Francisco, California, USA, Page 28

Three people were perhaps the most important to the construction of the Golden Gate Bridge: Joseph Strauss (1870–1938) the engineer, Irving Morrow (1884–1952) the architect, and Charles Ellis (1876–1949), who worked out the maths of the structure.

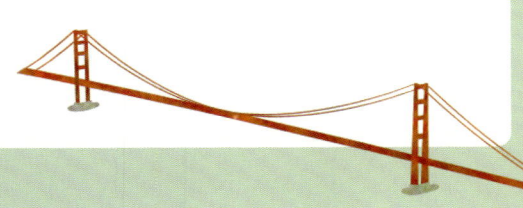

MILLAU VIADUCT
near Millau, France, Page 28

Norman Foster, who was born in 1936 and whose official title is Baron Foster of Thames Bank, was the architect of the Viaduct. Michel Virlogeux, who was born in 1946, was its structural engineer. Some of Foster's other completed projects include Hong Kong International Airport, Wembley Stadium in London and the transformation of the Reichstag in Berlin.

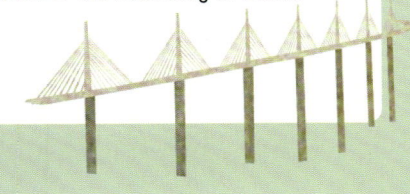

TOWER BRIDGE,
London, UK, Page 29

Tower Bridge was designed by Sir Horace Jones (1819–87), the City Architect, in collaboration with his engineer Sir John Barry (1836–1918). Barry was the youngest son of Sir Charles Barry, the architect of Big Ben.

BROOKLYN BRIDGE
New York City, NY, USA, Page 29

The original designer of the bridge, John Roebling (1806–69), died before construction started. Work was taken over by his son Washington Roebling (1837–1926), who became partially paralysed after breathing the compressed air in the *caissons* or underwater foundations of the bridge. His wife, Emily Roebling (1843–1903), managed the completion of the construction.

GREAT PYRAMID OF GIZA
near Cairo, Egypt, Pages 30–31

Pharaoh Khufu was the first pharaoh to build a pyramid at Giza. Little is known about him but it is believed that he ruled for about thirty years and had about fourteen children. He must have been a good organizer to have coordinated the building of the Great Pyramid!

TAJ MAHAL
Agra, India, Pages 32–35

Shah Jahan (1592–1666), one of the Mughal Emperors of India, commissioned the Taj Mahal. Shah Jahan loved the arts and ordered the building of many beautiful monuments; he was also a great military leader. The Taj Mahal was designed by a team of architects led by Ustad Ahmad Lahauri.

GREAT WALL OF CHINA
China, Pages 36–37

Built over 2,000 years by many architects, the Great Wall of China was originally made up of lots of different walls. This collection of walls did not become one Great Wall until Emperor Qin (259–210 BC). He is famous for his tomb, which is guarded by an army of terracotta (or clay) soldiers.

CHURCH OF THE LIGHT
Ibaraki, near Osaka, Japan, Pages 38–39

Tadao Ando was born in Osaka in 1941. He didn't go to university, working instead as a professional boxer, but he studied architecture by working as a carpenter and visiting buildings. His buildings, most of which are in Japan, are largely made of concrete and glass.

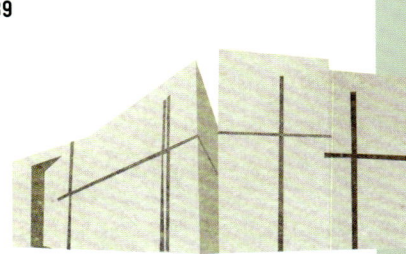

SYDNEY OPERA HOUSE
Sydney, Australia, Pages 40–41

Jørn Utzon was born in Copenhagen, Denmark, in 1918. Utzon was a keen sailor and his knowledge of shipbuilding gave him the inspiration for the Opera House roofs, which look like sails. He died in Copenhagen in 2008 at the age of ninety, having never visited the completed Opera House.

CHAMBER OF DEPUTIES, SECRETARIAT, SENATE, CATHEDRAL, PALACE OF JUSTICE AND NATIONAL THEATRE
Brasilia, Brazil, Pages 44–45

Oscar Niemeyer was born in 1907. He was a member of the Communist Party and when the military took over his country in 1964 he left Brazil for twenty years. Niemeyer died in 2012, at the age of 104, in Rio de Janeiro, Brazil.

SHANGHAI WORLD FINANCIAL CENTER
Shanghai, China, Page 46

This skyscraper was designed by the architecture firm Kohn Pederson Fox, founded in 1976. It was completed in 2008 and contains offices, hotels, shops and three observation decks. The building is known locally as 'the bottle opener' because of its shape.

AGBAR TOWER
Barcelona, Spain, Page 46

This tower is the headquarters of Agbar, the local water company in Barcelona. It was inspired by the architecture of Antoni Gaudí and by the nearby hills of Montserrat. The tower was designed by Jean Nouvel, who was born in 1945, and a company called b720, a team of architects from Barcelona. It was completed in 2005.

TELEVISION TOWER
Berlin, Germany, Page 46

The Berlin Television Tower was built to transmit German television and radio and still broadcasts more than fifty programmes today. The design, by Hermann Henselmann (1905–95), was inspired by the Russian satellite Sputnik. Fritz Dieter and Günter Franke were responsible for its construction, which was completed in 1969. In the middle of the sphere there is a revolving restaurant with a 360-degree view of Berlin.

TURNING TORSO
Malmö, Sweden, Page 46

The Turning Torso, the tallest building in Scandinavia, is a block of flats and offices. It was completed in 2005 by Spanish architect Santiago Calatrava, who was born in 1951 in Valencia, Spain. The design for the building is based on a sculpture, also by Calatrava, of a turning human body.

BIG BEN
London, UK, Page 46

Big Ben is the name of the largest bell inside the clock tower of the United Kingdom's Houses of Parliament. It has become the nickname of the tower, although the tower was officially renamed the Elizabeth Tower in 2012 to celebrate Queen Elizabeth II's sixty-year reign. It was completed in 1859. Charles Barry, the architect of the tower, was born in 1795 on Bridge Street, London, opposite the future site of Big Ben. He died in London in 1860.

PETRONAS TOWERS
Kuala Lumpur, Malaysia, Page 46

The twin towers of the Petronas building were built in 1996 as the headquarters of Malaysia's national petrol company, Petronas, and to house offices for other companies. Cesar Pelli, the architect of the towers, was born in Tucuman in northern Argentina in 1926 and now lives and works in the USA.

EMPIRE STATE BUILDING
New York City, NY, USA, Page 47

Completed in 1931, the Empire State Building was designed by William Lamb (1883–1952) as an office building. It is a very famous, iconic landmark not only in New York City but around the world.

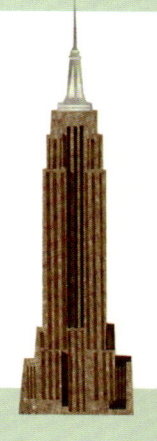

LEARN MORE ABOUT EACH BUILDING AND ITS ARCHITECT

TRANSAMERICA PYRAMID
San Francisco, California, USA, Page 47

Built as the headquarters for the Transamerica insurance company, the Transamerica Pyramid now houses the offices of about fifty different companies. The building was designed by William Pereira (1909–85) and it was completed in 1972. The shape of the building lets as much light as possible filter down to the streets below, which allows a grove of giant redwood trees to grow at its base.

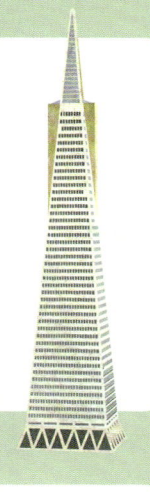

MOSCOW STATE UNIVERSITY
Moscow, Russia, Page 47

This university – the largest and oldest in Russia – was established in 1755 in Moscow and a new campus was completed in 1953. It was designed by Lev Rudnev (1885–1956). The building is known as one of the Seven Sisters, a name given to a group of skyscrapers built in Moscow between 1947 and 1953, which all look very similar.

BURJ KHALIFA
Dubai, United Arab Emirates, Page 47

The tallest building in the world (for now!), the Burj Khalifa was completed in 2010 and contains offices, flats and a hotel. The architecture firm Skidmore, Owings and Merrill was responsible for its construction; in particular Adrian Smith (born in 1944), the chief designer on the project, and William Baker (born in 1953), the structural and civil engineer.

LEANING TOWER
Pisa, Italy, Page 48

Construction of the Leaning Tower began in 1173 and wasn't completed until about 1360. Several architects are believed to have worked on the tower, including Bonanno Pisano, who is thought to have started the construction, and Giovanni di Simone.

SEAGRAM BUILDING
New York City, NY, USA, Page 48

Ludwig Mies van der Rohe, known as Mies, was born in Aachen, Germany, in 1886. He was the head of two important art and design colleges, one in Germany called the Bauhaus and another in Chicago, USA, which is now known as the Illinois Institute of Technology. Mies died in Chicago in 1969. He designed the Seagram Building in collaboration with Philip Johnson (1906–2005).

CCTV HEADQUARTERS
Beijing, China, Pages 48-49

This tower was designed by Dutch architect Rem Koolhaas (born in 1944) and other architects from his architecture firm, OMA (Office for Metropolitan Architecture). Koolhaas also likes to write books on architecture; the most famous is called *Delirious New York*.

LONDON BRIDGE TOWER (OR 'THE SHARD')
London, UK, Page 49

The London Bridge Tower was completed by the firm of the Italian architect Renzo Piano, who also designed the Georges Pompidou Centre (see pages 10–11) and the Kansai International Airport in Japan.

FALLINGWATER
Bear Run, Pennsylvania, USA, Pages 50-53

Frank Lloyd Wright was born in Wisconsin, USA, in 1867, and died in Arizona, USA, in 1959. He was an architect, interior designer and writer, and believed in designing things that fitted in well with their surroundings and environment. He designed many buildings and structures, including the Guggenheim Museum in New York City, USA.

CHRYSLER BUILDING
New York City, NY, USA, Pages 54-55

The Chrysler Building was built by William Van Alen, who was born in New York City, USA, in 1883 and died also in New York in 1954. As a student he won an architecture prize, and as a result went to study at the École des Beaux-Arts in Paris. After his death, a fund was set up in his name, which still awards architecture scholarships today.

WALT DISNEY CONCERT HALL
Los Angeles, California, USA, Pages 56-57

Frank Gehry was born in Toronto, Canada, in 1929. His recent buildings, like the Guggenheim Museum in Bilbao, Spain, are famous for their complicated, curving walls. Gehry is a big ice hockey fan.

Dedicated to my two little peepers,
Jack Featherpeck and Sam Ruffbreast

I should like to thank several very dear friends, without whom this remarkable book would never have happened:

Stella "Pigeon Whisperer" Gurney, highly esteemed by pigeonkind as a human friend, ambassador and translator of tricky pigeon phrases.

Natsko Seki, for her stunning rendition of my favourite buildings, and rather flattering portrayal of yours truly.

Hélène Gallois Montbrun - my kind, helpful and open-minded editor, who spoke to me in her office all those months ago and has worked untiringly with me ever since.

Rachel Williams, a dear human friend of mine and Elsie's who first had the idea that we reveal our true selves to humans by way of a book.

And finally, Amanda Renshaw, who gave this book wings, and Julia Hasting, Sandra Zellmer and Rebecca Price who gave it beauty.

Phaidon Press Limited
Regent's Wharf
All Saints Street
London N1 9PA

www.phaidon.com

First published 2013
© 2013 Phaidon Press Limited

ISBN 978 0 7148 6353 5 (UK edition)
004-0913

A CIP catalogue record for this book is available from the British Library.

All rights reserved. No part of this publication may be reproduced, stored in a retrieval system or transmitted, in any form or by any means, electronic, mechanical, photocopying, recording or otherwise, without the written permission of Phaidon Press Limited.

Illustrations by Natsko Seki

Designed by Julia Hasting with Sandra Zellmer

Printed in China

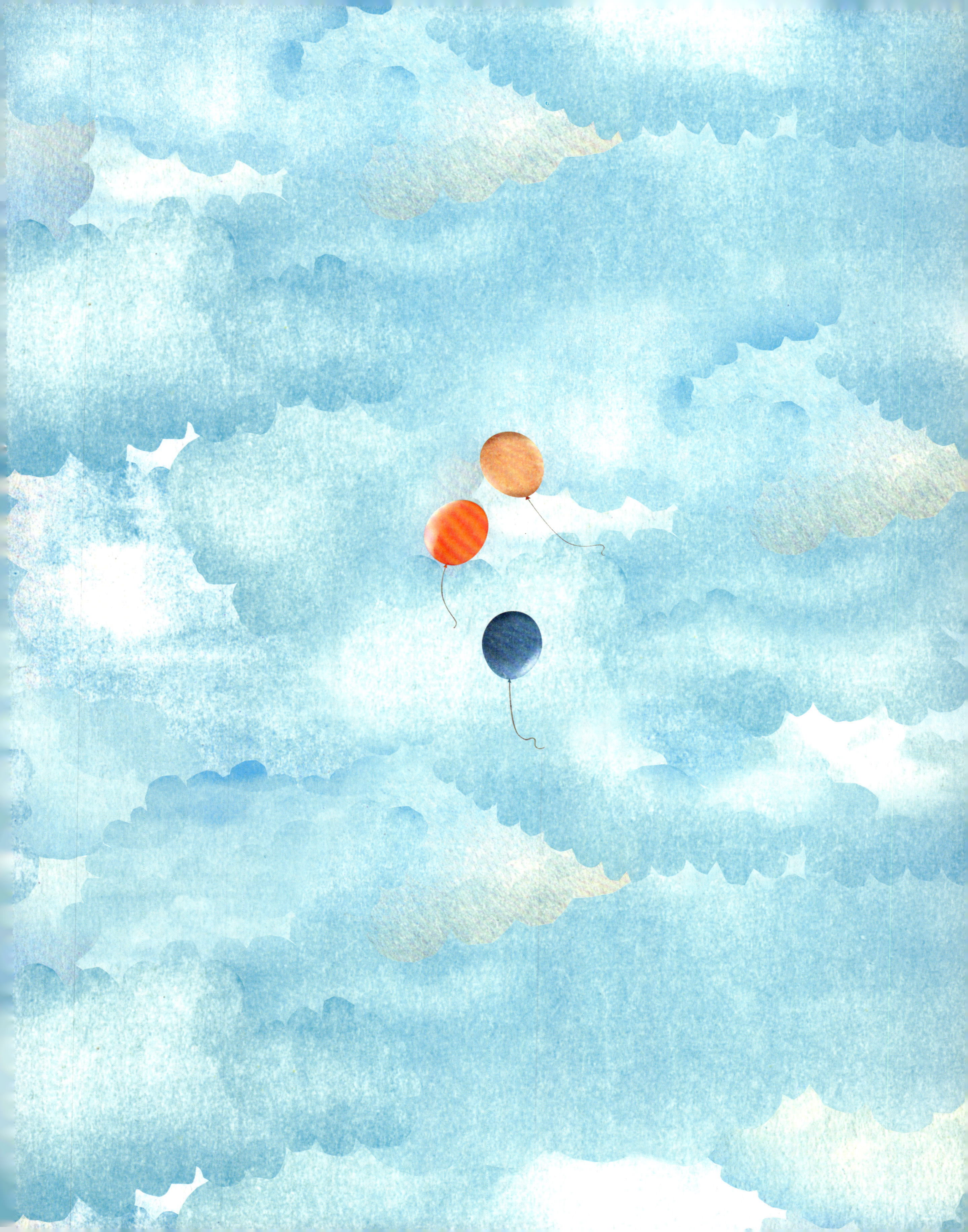